For CAROL
Sche is fayr as is
the Rose
in May.

CLARION BOOKS
Ticknor & Fields, a Houghton Mifflin Company

Copyright ©1982 by Donald Carrick

Printed in the U.S.A.

Library of Congress Cataloging in Publication Data

Carrick, Donald.
Harald and the giant knight.
Summary: When a group of knights decide to use his father's farm
for their spring training, Harald and his family must take desperate
measures to get the troublesome knights off their land.
[1.Knights and knighthood—Fiction]   I.Title
PZ7.C2345Har   [E]   81-10243   ISBN 0-89919-060-X   AACR2

H 10 9 8 7 6 5 4 3 2

HARALD AND THE GIANT KNIGHT

BY DONALD CARRICK

CLARION BOOKS
TICKNOR & FIELDS : A HOUGHTON MIFFLIN COMPANY
NEW YORK

Harald lived with his mother, Helga, and his father, Walter, in the valley which spread beneath the castle.

The valley was owned by a baron who lived in the castle, surrounded by his knights. All the farmers in the valley had to give the Baron part of

their crops. He, in turn, allowed them to farm his land. Harald's family had farmed the same land for as long as anyone could remember.

Harald's father was a weaver as well as a farmer. He wove eel traps, screens, hats, fences, chairs, and every manner of basket.

One spring morning Harald climbed up to the castle with baskets his father had woven for the castle kitchen. Harald went to the castle as often as he could.

After he delivered the baskets, he wandered through the passageways, exploring the wondrous stone chambers. Many were larger than his home.

Harald was especially fond of the Baron's knights. Knights were different from other folk. They were huge, scarred men who wore leather and metal clothes covered by bright tunics. The knights spoke with deep voices and their clothing creaked and clanked as they walked by. Harald burned to be one of them.

Harald loved the jousts when two knights fought. Best of all were the tournaments. Then he could watch all the Baron's knights clash with all the knights from another castle in a mock battle. Nothing made Harald happier than to see the galloping horses and the swirling banners, and to hear the clang of sword against shield.

On this particular morning the Baron announced that it was time to begin training for the summer tournaments. A great cheer went up from the knights. They were restless after the long winter they had spent inside the castle.

As Harald walked home, he wished he could train with them.

The next morning, a terrible racket woke Harald. He ran outside to
find his father in a fit. Men from the castle were swarming all over their
farm. Horns blew. Kettledrums boomed. Tents were going up.

"What's happening?" Harald asked.

"The knights' regular practice fields are flooded, so they've come here
to train," his father said.

Harald watched as knights strutted about, shouting a thousand orders.

"We are ruined," groaned Walter. "With all this foolish practice on our fields, how can we plant the spring crops?"

Harald understood how his father felt. Without a harvest, his family would have no food and could not pay the Baron for the use of his land. But at the same time, it was Harald's dream come true. All the knights were right here on his family's farm!

Walter's fields were transformed into a jousting arena in which the
knights galloped about on large horses and practiced with their lances.

Since no farming could be done, Harald spent all his time at the knights' camp. Soon he was helping with the horses and tending the fires. Perhaps there was a chance for him to become a knight after all.

The knights' presence changed everything on the farm. There were no more eggs to collect because the constant noise caused the chickens to stop laying. The pigs grew nervous and lost weight.

Harald could not believe it when knights tested their swords by chopping into his father's carefully tended fruit trees. The stone boundary fences his grandfather had built were broken and scattered.

The knights had huge appetites. To fill the camp cookpots they simply took what they wanted from Walter and the other valley farmers. Chickens, ducks, pigs, and goats disappeared in their stewpots and on the roasting spits.

Harald was shocked. He had always thought knights were strong, brave men who spent their time helping people. Instead, he saw them ruin the land and plunder the farms like thieves.

Walter was pleased when Harald announced one day that he was no longer going to the camp. Harald had lost his taste for the knightly life.

To save what little food they had left, Helga gathered it together and put it in a sack. When it was dark, Harald went with his father to hide it. They carried the food down a small path past the knights' camp to a secret cave. Harald had discovered the cave one day last summer while he was picking berries. They hid the food on a high ledge.

When they returned home, no one could sleep so they sat together around their small fire. There seemed to be no answer to their problem.

"If I were big, I'd thrash all the knights and send them running," said Harald. "It's the only thing they understand."

"No one is big enough to do that," answered Helga, "except another knight."

Walter said nothing, but his hands began weaving. The giant shadows his father cast on the wall gave Harald an idea.

"I know how we can get rid of the knights!" he said.

His father stopped weaving. "What do you mean, son?" he asked.

"Well, why can't we make a knight to frighten them?"

"And just how would we do that, Harald?" asked Helga.

"Father is a master weaver, isn't he? He can weave anything. Why can't he weave a giant knight?"

A smile spread over Walter's face. "Let's hear more," he said.

Excitedly they talked late into the night as idea led to idea. By morning they had a plan.

From the next day on, Harald's family spent all their time at the cave weaving their giant. Harald made trip after trip to the cave, bringing Walter great bundles of reeds.

One afternoon rabbit hunters from the camp almost discovered the cave as Harald was about to enter.

"Where are you bound with that bundle, lad?" called the leader, coming closer.

Harald knew that once the dogs got near the entrance to the cave, all would be lost. "Oh, I'm on my way to build a rabbit hutch," he replied, thinking quickly.

"Rabbits! What rabbits?" demanded the hunters.

"The rabbits in the thicket down the ravine. It's full of them," said Harald.

"Well lad, we'll just take a look at this thicket of yours," said the leader, and the hunters marched off.

With each bundle of Harald's reeds, the basket knight grew larger. Harald was very proud of his father's skill. He was sure nothing this large had ever been woven.

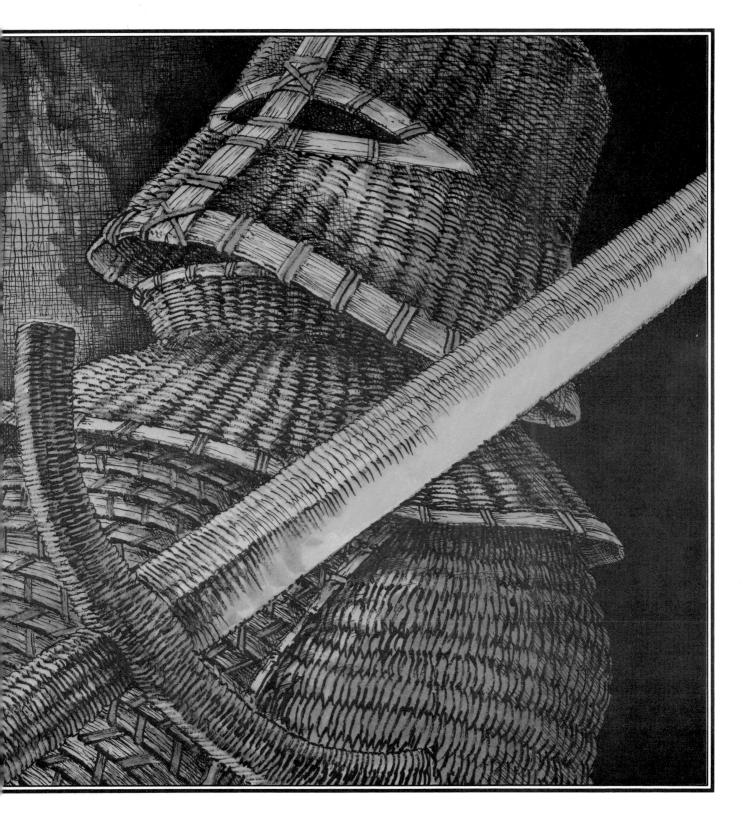

"By daylight, he will probably look rather patchy," Walter said. "But by night, after the knights have finished drinking and are asleep, our knight should be very frightening."

Helga decided to make a cape for him.

Finally the giant basket knight was finished. He was almost too large to squeeze through the cave entrance. Carefully they mounted the creature on Patience, their old plow horse, and tied it down.

Walter led Patience down the narrow trail. The knight looked huge but weighed so little that each draft from the valley caught it like a sail. Harald clung to a rope to steady the creature.

At one spot the trees were so close they almost pushed the basket giant off Patience's back. When the knight swayed back and forth it looked even more ghost-like.

"These paths were not made for giants," Harald whispered.

Each small farm along the way had a dog that barked as the giant drew near. Harald started to shiver. What if they were discovered? Fortunately no one woke.

When they arrived at the edge of camp, the knights were all asleep.

It was Harald's task to enter the camp and untie the horses. He slipped quietly past the tents full of snoring knights. By day he knew the camp, but by night it all seemed different. One mistake could ruin everything.

At last he found the horses and with trembling hands untied the knots. The freed horses began to wander through the camp.

In the light of the early moon, Harald saw the giant loom above the trees.

The moment he appeared, Walter and Helga began a horrific clamor. She clanged pots while he made loud, moaning sounds through a long wooden tube.

That was the signal for Harald to dart from tent to tent, pulling up tent pegs. One after another, the tents collapsed on the sleeping knights.

The bewildered knights awoke in the dark, blanketed by the heavy tents. As they groped free, they tripped over ropes and cracked their shins on tent poles.

Once they were in the open, the mob of bruised, half-clothed knights was startled by the sight of the giant. It seemed to be walking over the trees. And it began to shout at them in a deep, creaky voice.

"AWAY WITH YOU. AWAY FROM THE GRAVES OF MY FOREFA-THERS. BEGONE, ALL OF YOU, BEFORE THE NEW DAY DAWNS!"

Then, suddenly, the swaying knight seemed to disappear from the sky. The frightened knights were left standing in the shambles of the camp. Actually, the giant had fallen from Patience's back and she trotted away, dragging him behind.

Harald caught up with his parents who were close on Patience's heels. They were busy picking up the bits and pieces that were falling from the giant. There was no time to wonder if their plan had worked until they reached the cave.

Dumbfounded, the knights milled about the camp gathering their wits and their horses. No trace of the ghostly giant could be found.

No one wanted to mention the ghost's warning, but one knight had the courage to say, "This camp is a wreck. I think it's time to leave."

"Let's go back to the castle," said a second.

A great sigh of relief came from all sides. Not one knight wanted to stay on and risk seeing the giant again.

Shortly after sunrise Harald, Helga, and Walter watched the band of knights make their way slowly up the hill toward the castle. Helga and Walter hugged each other and cried with relief. Harald, who could not contain himself, jumped for joy.

After a great deal of work, the three of them cleared their fields and planted crops. That fall their harvest was not as big as usual, but it was enough to pay the Baron and feed themselves through the winter.

The next spring Harald and his father were planting once again.

"Listen to what the wind brings us from down the valley," said Walter.

They could hear a faint clanging from the knights at practice on the Baron's field. This time they were but pleasant tinkles to Harald's ears.

Nearby stood a familiar figure. It was a scarecrow, fashioned from the giant's reeds. As it turned with the wind, it almost seemed to smile.